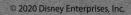

Illustrated by Jerrod Maruyama
© 2020 Disney Enterprises, Inc. All rights reserved.

Customer Service: 1-877-277-9441 or customerservice@pikidsmedia.com

Published by PI Kids, an imprint of Phoenix International Publications, Inc.

8501 West Higgins Road   59 Gloucester Place
Chicago, Illinois 60631   London W1U 8JJ

PI Kids is a trademark of Phoenix International Publications, Inc., and is registered in the United States.

www.pikidsmedia.com

ISBN: 978-1-5037-5497-3

Morty Tells the Truth

A STORY ABOUT HONESTY

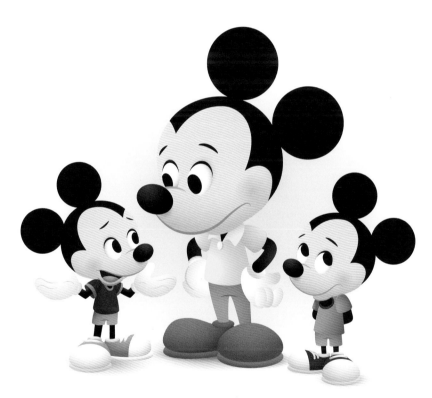

pi kids ®

An imprint of Phoenix International Publications, Inc.

Chicago • London • New York • Hamburg • Mexico City • Sydney

Morty and Ferdie are having some fun playing with **sticky**, **icky** "goo."

"We better put our backpacks and stuff away, so we don't make a **mess**," says Ferdie.

But Morty
doesn't listen.

"Look at this, Ferdie!" shouts Morty. "I made a volcano and it's about to erupt! **Run**!"

The goo spreads everywhere, just like lava! It seeps
under Morty's backpack—and covers his **library book**.

Kaboom!

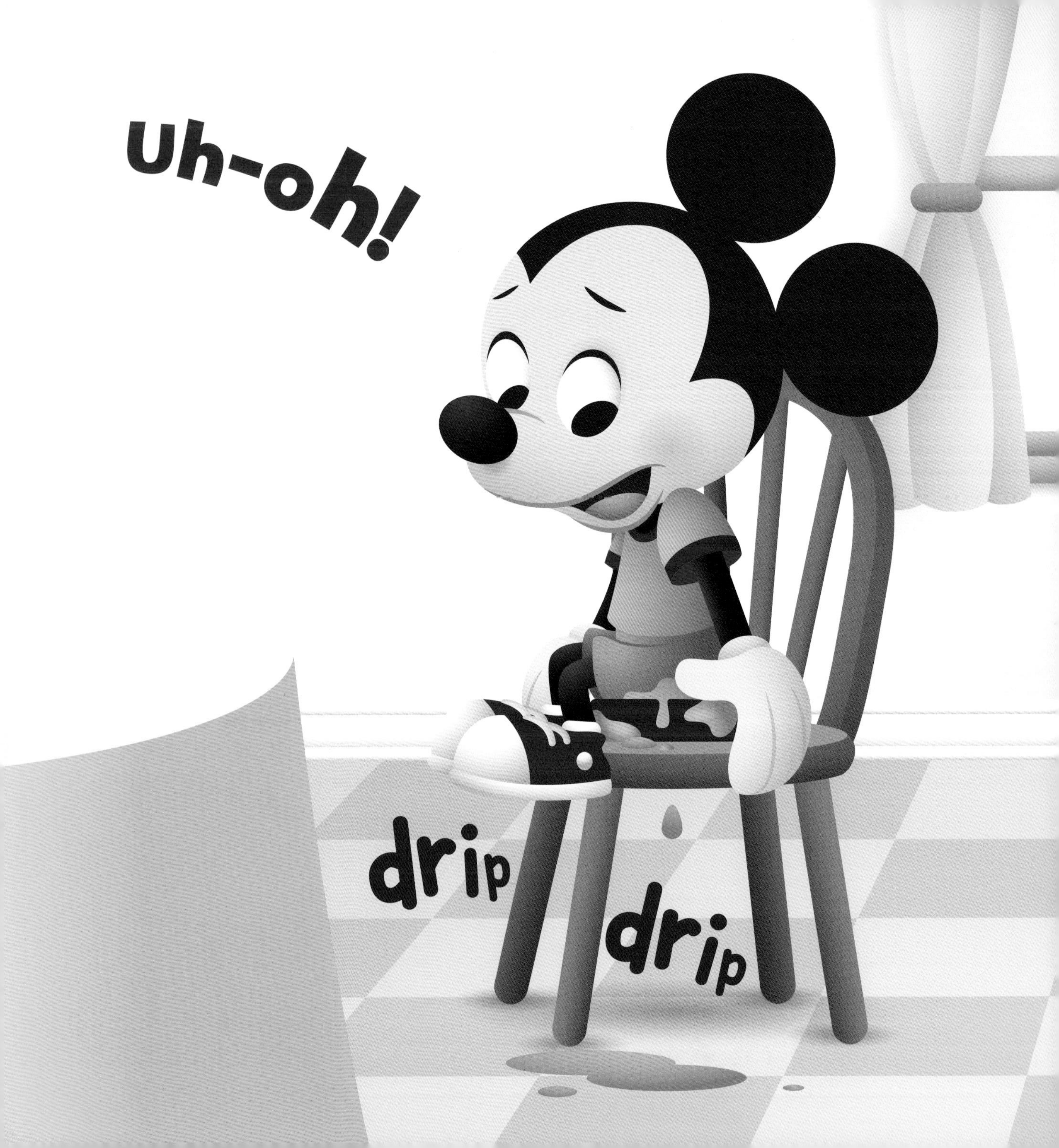

Uh-oh!
drip
drip

I can't let
Ferdie see the **mess**
I made of my *library*
book, Morty thinks.
He quickly sits
on the goo-covered
book to hide it.

The next morning, Morty tells his Uncle Mickey that he can't find his **library book**.

"Have you seen it, Ferdie?" asks Mickey.

"Nope," says Ferdie. "But **I'll help** you and Morty look."

Morty, Ferdie, and Mickey search through the toy chest and explore under the bed. They come up **empty-handed**.

"Time for school," says Mickey. "I'll keep looking for your **book**."

"We were playing outside last night," says Ferdie. "Maybe it's out there."

While the boys are at school, Goofy comes over to help Mickey search.

"I don't see the **book** anywhere," says Mickey.

"We'll find it," says Goofy. "I'll **dig up every inch** of your backyard if I have to!"

At school, Morty tells his teacher that the **book** is lost.

"Oh, dear," says Ms. Clarabelle. "I'm sure the class will help you look."

Morty's friends search their **classroom**,

the **art room**,

the **music room**,

and the **playground**,

but no one can find the book.

When Morty gets home, Mickey can tell he is **sad**.

"Guess you didn't find the book at school," Mickey says. "Goofy and I didn't find it here, either. But don't worry. Donald said he would come over and **help you look** some more."

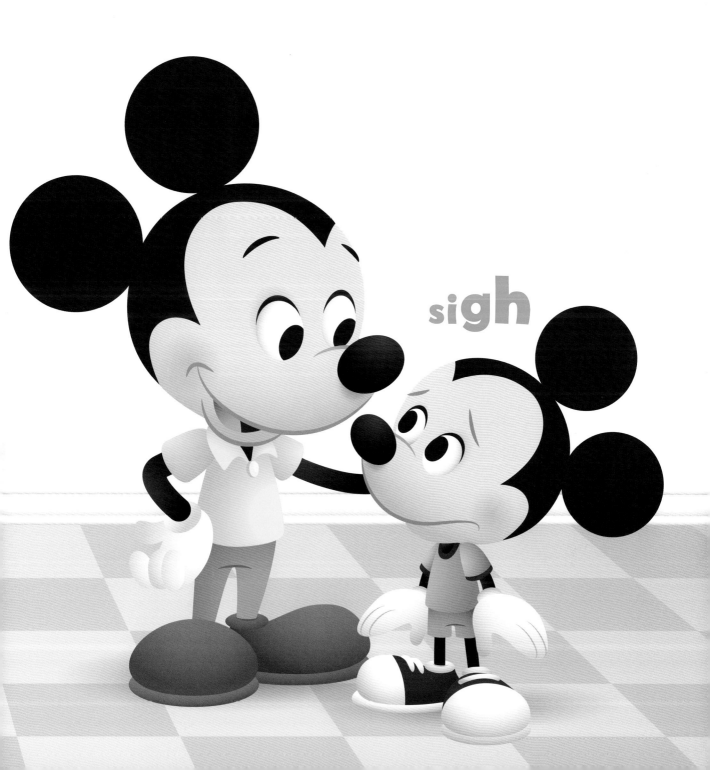

Donald takes Morty to retrace all of his steps from yesterday. They walk to and from the school, looking high...

...and low,

from the top of the slide to the bottom of the swing set. But still, no book.

The next day at school, Mr. Goodman the custodian finds Ferdie.

"I think this **book** belongs to your brother, Morty," he says. "His name is the last one on the library card."

drip

"Wow!" says Ferdie. "Where did you find it? We've been looking everywhere."

"I found it in the trash can by the playground," says Mr. Goodman.

Ferdie's eyes grow **wide** with surprise.

When Ferdie sees Morty,
he hands him the **goo**-covered
book.

"You'll never guess where
this was found," says Ferdie.

drip

Squish

"In the trash can by the playground," says Morty, sighing sadly. **"I know...**

...because I'm the one who put it in there."

When the boys get home, Morty shows Mickey the damaged **book**.

"Why did you lie to us?" asks Ferdie.

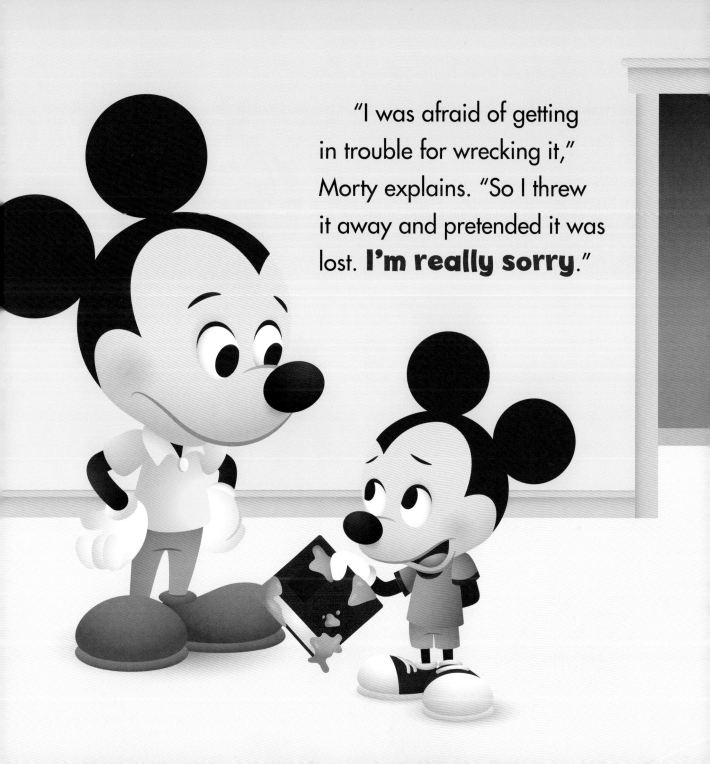

"I was afraid of getting in trouble for wrecking it," Morty explains. "So I threw it away and pretended it was lost. **I'm really sorry**."

"A lot of people helped you look for that **book**," says Mickey.

"I'm going to say **I'm sorry** to each of them," says Morty.

"And I'll use my allowance money to pay for a brand-new **book**."

"I'm proud of you for making the right decision," says Mickey. "You can never go wrong by being honest."

Morty agrees: **It's better to tell the truth!**